# Rabbit
# on the Run

Written by Alex Lane

Illustrated by Laura Hughes

OXFORD

UNIVERSITY PRESS

Rabbit was quick.

3

Rabbit was on the run.

Hang on!

4

5

Rabbit shot off.

Rabbit ran and ran.

Rabbit had a nap.

Rabbit got up.

Rabbit was in a rush.

## Retell the story

**Once upon a time...**

**The end.**